SECRET HOLES

SECRET HOLES

by

Pansie Hart Flood

illustrated by

Felicia Marshall

Carolrhoda Books, Inc. / Minneapolis

Carolrhoda Books, Inc.
A division of Lerner Publishing Group
241 First Avenue North
Minneapolis, MN 55401 U.S.A.

Website address: www.lernerbooks.com

Library of Congress Cataloging-in-Publication Data

Flood, Pansie Hart.
    Secret holes / by Pansie Hart Flood ; illustrated by Felicia Marshall.
        p.   cm.
    Summary: Ten-year-old Sylvia has just discovered that her centenarian best
friend is also her great-grandmother, and together they pursue discoveries yet to
come.
    ISBN: 0–87614–923–9 (lib. bdg. : alk. paper)
    [1. Family life—South Carolina—Fiction. 2. Great-grandmothers—Fiction.
3. Best friends—Fiction. 4. Old age—Fiction. 5. African Americans—Fiction.
6. South Carolina—Fiction.] I. Marshall, Felicia, ill. II. Title.
PZ7.F66185 Se 2003
[Fic]—dc21   2002151965

Manufactured in the United States of America
1 2 3 4 5 6 – SB – 08 07 06 05 04 03

In memory of my beloved grandmother, whose existence inspired me to create the character Miz Lula Maye

Pearlie Mae Reaves Wallace
1892–2000

Also, for Merrill, Jasmine, and Joey for unconditional love, support, patience, and belief in my writing

Contents

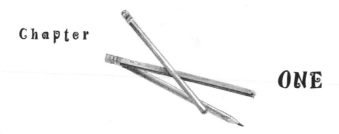

Chapter ONE

The

Next

Day

I knew I musta been dreamin', 'cause I couldn't feel myself breathing. If you ain't dreamin', you can feel yourself breathing, 'cause things is happening for real. When you're dreamin', you don't even know you's alive.

My mind was involved in a serious dream. I think it was about Florida. That's where I used to live. A couple of months ago, me and my momma packed up all our belongings, got on a bus, and ended up here in Wakeview, South

Carolina, way deep down in the country.

I rolled over on my back. Zap! went my Florida dream right then and there. I was chewing like a cow when I opened my eyes. I bet I looked just like Jack Jr. looked the day before on the couch, napping after stuffing himself silly with Sunday dinner. Jack Jr. is the family clown. He's always up to something for a laugh.

I'd just found out on Sunday that Jack Jr. is my cousin. Since my momma and me landed in Wakeview at the start of summer, Jack Jr. had just been a friend who lived on Pearle Road. So findin' out he's family was quite a surprise.

Even though Cousin Jack Jr. is about five times older than I am, we have something else in common besides living on Pearle Road and bein' family. We both loves Miz Lula Maye. Miz Lula Maye is a lady who lives down at the end of Pearle Road, and she and I are the bestest friends in the whole wide world. And just because she turned one hundred years old not too long ago, doesn't matter to me. Miz Lula Maye is a whole lot of fun.

Anyway, back to Sunday. Sunday, my life went

through some major changes. Findin' out that Jack Jr. is my cousin was the last thing that came tumblin' out of the closet Sunday.

The first shocker of the day was this man who showed up. I called him Mr. Mystery Man. Come to find out this man was or is my daddy. For all of my life, ten years to be exact, I was told that my daddy was dead. Well, since Sunday, he sho' ain't dead no more. He is about as alive as the catfish swimming around on the muddy bottom of Catfish Creek.

I was thinking about my new daddy when I heard my momma come out of the bathroom. She leaves for work in Miz Lula Maye's fields shortly before sunrise every day but Sunday. Farmers round here in Wakeview likes to get an extra early start to beat the heat.

I pulled the sheet up over my head so she couldn't see I was awake. Momma knew good and well that I was still kinda mad at her. She knew my daddy was alive. I couldn't understand why she didn't tell me the truth. Why did she tell me a tale? I wondered . . . her daughter, her only child.

After I found out about my daddy, my momma claimed that she and I was gonna have a long talk. But did we? No! My momma has always been good at puttin' off talk about her past. All those years, I'd always felt there was somethin' missing in my life. "'Cause of Momma's secrets," I whispered to myself under my sheets.

There ought to be a law that says when children ask questions, they must get answers. Yes, answers, right then and there! No waiting until mommas get ready. Hey now, that's my kinda law. The law should probably say something about tellin' the truth, too.

Don't get me wrong. I loves my momma. She works twice as hard out in the hot fields croppin' peppers. Without Momma, I honestly don't know where I'd be.

After Momma left for work, I sat up in bed wondering about things. "Yesterday changed everything," I said, blowing with my cheeks puffed like Dizzy Gillespie playin' the trumpet. Maybe today might be a good day to sit down and figure out all this family business on paper, I thought.

"I need something to write on and something

to write with," I announced to myself. "Hmmm," I considered with my fingers over my mouth.

I jumped out of bed and fumbled through my closet, pushing boxes to the side. The boxes had been in there all summer, since we moved in. Hadn't been no need for anything in 'em 'cause I been busy with Miz Lula Maye pretty much since I got here.

I found a box labeled School Stuff. Brown packing tape was still taped all around and over the box. It had been taped for so long in this heat that it didn't want to come off. I had to use my momma's scissors to cut it open. I pulled out several sheets of paper. Then I zipped open a purple pencil bag and searched for two pencils with good erasers. I pressed a piece of tape back over the box and slid it back into my junky closet.

I had an idea. Miz Lula Maye gets this magazine about famous black people. It's called *Ebony*. I think she said her daughter Miz Peaches bought her a subscription. I remembered seeing a drawing of a family tree in one of *Ebony*'s magazines. It showed how people in a family were related to each other by making 'em all branches on a tree. I reckoned I

knew enough to start drawin' a family tree.

At the top of the page I wrote "Sylvia Freeman's Family Tree—Summer of 1978." Now, I wondered, should my name and birth date be at the top of the tree or the bottom? Should it be a fat, round-lookin' tree? Or should it be a tall, slender-lookin' tree? Should the tree have leaves? Or should I draw a Charlie Brown-lookin' tree with just branches and no leaves?

"Oh, Lord!" I sighed. This tree drawing activity was already turning out to be more difficult than planned.

I didn't know whether it was right or wrong, but I decided to put my name (Sylvia Frances Freeman) and birthday (September 29, 1967) at the bottom of the tree.

On the right side, I wrote down Momma's name (Marie Freeman) and her birthday (May 6, 1948). The only other people on Momma's side that I knew of was Grandma and Grandpa Freeman. They both died in a house fire when she was little. I didn't know their birthdays. In fact, I didn't even know their first names, so I left those spaces blank.

Up until Sunday, that was my whole family tree. It wasn't really even a tree. It was more like a twig or a switch that makes good spankin' material.

On the left side, I wrote Mr. Mystery Man's name: Jonathan Maye. Then I stared at it for a long time. I still couldn't believe I had a daddy.

My momma had me back when Mr. Jonathan was fighting in the Vietnam War. But they weren't married, and she never wrote to him and told him she was having a baby. The reason Mr. Jonathan showed up on Pearle Road didn't have a thing to do with me. He grew up on Pearle Road and wanted to pay a surprise visit to Miz Lula Maye. But once he recognized Momma, it all came out.

This brings me to maybe the biggest surprise of all. Mr. Jonathan is Miz Lula Maye's grandson. She raised Mr. Jonathan because his momma, Miz Lula Maye's daughter, died when he was born. So guess what that means? That's right! My best friend, Miz Lula Maye, is also my great-grandma, and that makes us closer than two peas in a pod. Even though some parts of this terror is bad, some parts is extra-special good.

I added Miz Lula Maye's name and birthday (July 21, 1878) to my family tree. Above her name I wrote in big letters "GREAT-GRANDMA & BEST FRIEND."

Underneath Miz Lula Maye's name, I drew six lines for her children. I met them at Miz Lula Maye's one-hundredth birthday party. I also met their kids and grandkids. The only name I could remember from all those people was Miz Peaches, who was Miz Lula Maye's daughter. So I wrote down her name and left the rest blank. I made a bubble for the three children Miz Lula Maye had that died. I knew that one of them was Mr. Jonathan's momma, but I couldn't remember her name, either.

And where was I supposed to put silly-acting Cousin Jack Jr.? I wasn't sure, so I wrote his name beside the tree and drew a circle around it with a question mark.

Momma's side of the tree looked a bit scarce. Unfortunately, unless she ever decided to have that long talk, her side would be empty. It's always been that way with us—no family, I mean.

Other kids I knew back in Florida would get together with their families for Thanksgiving and Christmas and other times, too. But Momma and me, well it would just be Momma and me.

This year, for the first time, things are gonna be different, I told myself. I've got a new daddy, a new great-grandma/best friend, and Cousin Jack Jr. Lord only knows how many others from Miz Lula Maye's family will come home for the holidays. I looked at my family tree and started dreamin' again. Only this time, it was a daydream, 'cause I knew I was awake.

At Thanksgiving, there would be lots of grub (you know it) and lots of family sitting around a big, long table. Maybe everybody would take turns saying grace or saying what they were thankful for. Just like families do on TV.

At Christmas, we'd have a bunch of presents under a big tree with big colorful lights. Ornaments! Yes, Miz Lula Maye and I would make a million ornaments for my first Christmas tree with my new family. And we'd pop popcorn and put it on strings and hang 'em on the tree. And maybe it would snow. And maybe we'd all sit around together on Christmas Eve and sing Christmas carols and drink eggnog and bake cookies. And maybe we'd all be smiling on the outside and the inside.

Chapter  TWO

Still

Best Friends?

I heard the mail truck at about ten o'clock. The mail didn't usually come that early on Mondays. I jumped out of bed and peeped between the blinds in my window to be sure. It's my job to deliver the mail to Miz Lula Maye. I check all the mailboxes at the road every day except Sundays, and that's because the mail doesn't run on Sundays.

I thought twice about going over to Miz Lula Maye's. After Sunday's circus of events, I wasn't sure about me and her anymore. I knew how to be her best friend, but I didn't know if I knew how to be her great-granddaughter. But goin' to Miz Lula Maye's house every day has gotten to be a habit. Things just don't seem right if I don't visit. So I had to get over what was bothering me.

I took a quick shower. Then I put on a white tank top and a pair of seersucker pink and white shorts. Both needed ironing, but that's something I rarely do. I don't really see a need for ironing clothes unless I'm going somewhere. Besides, don't nobody round here cares if my clothes is ironed or wrinkled. At least my clothes do match.

I grabbed Miz Lula Maye's mail from her mailbox and trotted off down Pearle Road. I thinks Miz Lula Maye owns everything on Pearle Road. That's probably why her house sits straight at the end of it. It's kinda like an important person (a king or a queen) who sits at the head of a table or on the throne. Yeah, that's Miz Lula Maye.

Miz Lula Maye rents out one of her houses to Momma and me. Jack Jr. lives in the other one, next door to Miz Lula Maye. He does a good job takin' care of her and helpin' out with her fields. Right across the road from Momma and me is the Juke Joint. The Juke Joint is Jack Jr.'s nightclub, and it's one hoppin' place. I think it must be the only place in South Carolina for grown folks to go drinkin' and dancin'. Jack Jr. would never admit the Juke Joint is not his own establishment, but I think it belongs to Miz Lula Maye.

It hadn't rained in a few days, so the road was super dry. Each step I took kicked up a cloud of gray-brownish dust. According to Miz Lula Maye, the dirt around here is mixed with some clay or something. That's why when it gets real hot and dry, dust kicks up everywhere.

Another thing I've noticed about Wakeview is that it stinks. Smells rusty and rotten all the time. Farmers mix animal poop in the soil. No wonder! That's why it stinks! Miz Lula Maye says it's called manure when farmers mix poop (mostly cow poop) with soil. She says cow manure makes the soil dark and rich. It grows a strong, healthy crop of mostly anything you plants. That may be true, but on hot, sticky days, especially before a storm, it reeks! Sometimes I have to hold my breath.

Miz Lula Maye was rockin' on her front porch. I could see her smiling once she spotted me. When I'm around Miz Lula Maye, all the stinky smells, dirty dust, and anything else that's bothering me kinda disappears. Miz Lula Maye is so beautiful to be one hundred years old. She wears her long, silky straight hair in two ponytails like an Indian doll. Her smooth, brown skin barely has wrinkles. Miz Lula Maye is just one amazing person in my eyes.

"Morning, Sylvia!" Miz Lula Maye said and chuckled with a happy-to-see-you smile.

"Well, hello, Sylvia!" A sound, the man sound of Mr. Jonathan's voice, came from the screen door. I hadn't even seen him standing there.

"Hey, ya'll," I said in a low but pleasant voice. I was hoping he wouldn't still be there. Well, sike! Yes, I was. Even though he was my daddy 'n all, I didn't really know him. I mean, I didn't know him well enough to feel right being with him by myself. Besides, he acted and talked so PROPER. He used all those big city words like rich folks from up North. For instance, yesterday he said he was elated to be back home. What in the world is elated?

The only person I'm used to sharing Miz Lula Maye with is Jack Jr. Oh, yeah, and her nine or so scrawny cats. Actually, Miz Lula Maye's cats aren't scrawny. I just like callin' 'em that. Miz Lula Maye's cats are fat and healthy looking. You would be, too, if you were fed like kings and queens.

It dawned on me that I left Miz Lula Maye's cats off the family tree. She treats her cats like they's her children. When I gets back home, I thought, I'll add 'em to the tree under Miz Lula Maye's name. Or maybe I'll just add their paws underneath the tree along the roots and make it look like they're trying to climb up the tree.

"Did you sleep well last night? Yesterday was certainly a humdinger of a day, wasn't it?" said you-know-who. I hoped he wouldn't start running off at the mouth too much. I didn't know that I was ready to hear any more surprising news. It was too early in the day for conversating, anyhow, at least with him.

"Have you had anything to eat yet?" Miz Lula Maye asked.

"No, ma'am," I said with a hungry grin.

And of course she said, "Well, let's get you something to eat. It's pert near lunchtime."

Still Best Friends?

Mr. Jonathan opened the screen door for me and Miz Lula Maye. He is so PROPER. I wonder where did he get his PROPER training? He probably got it from being in the army. From what I hears, those guys go through some tough training in boot camp.

Miz Lula Maye and me headed straight to the kitchen. Mr. Jonathan stayed outside on the front porch. Good! I thought. Ain't no sense in him hangin' around us womenfolks or watchin' me eat.

From breakfast, Miz Lula Maye had some leftover scrambled eggs mixed with hog brains. I wasn't too sure about eating hog brains, but all I could taste was eggs and bacon grease. To me, I guess, fried hog brains taste just like scrambled eggs. That's probably good because when you eatin' somebody's brains, it's best not to think about it.

Miz Lula Maye wasn't satisfied with me just eating fried hog brains. "Come on over here, Sylvia, and learns how to make these fresh onion fritters," she said.

I reckoned we still best friends. I smiled all

inside my body as I listened to her speak the recipe from memory. She has recipes written down, but can't nobody follows 'em but her. It's not that you can't read her handwriting. It's the language and the words. Everything is written in shorthand. Kinda like a secret code.

First she poured cornmeal in a mixing bowl. Then she added one egg, some milk, and some sugar. Miz Lula Maye let me mix the batter while she cut up slices of fresh long spring onions from her garden. Next she fried the onions in a small spider (that's what she calls a frying pan) with some butter and a dab of bacon grease.

"Sylvia, is your batter ready for me to add these onions?" Miz Lula Maye asked.

"I think so," I answered in an unsure voice. The batter was mixed, but it looked lumpy.

Miz Lula Maye peered into the bowl. "It's hard getting all the lumps out of cornmeal. They'll all cook out, anyway," she said. Then she added the onions and some dried herbs from her garden that looked like grass and weeds.

Miz Lula Maye scooped up a half measuring cup of batter and poured it into the hot spider.

Then she cooked it just like my momma cooks pancakes. Actually, these things looked like pancakes, but because there was stuff mixed inside, I think that's why they're called fritters. Then, too, I've never had pancakes made out of cornmeal. So maybe fritters are only made of cornmeal, and pancakes are only made of flour.

We sat down at the kitchen table to eat. Miz Lula Maye gave me two fritters. They looked good. Then before I could say anything, she spooned some of her own homemade strawberry preserves on top of my fritters. They didn't look so good anymore.

I wasn't exactly sure how all this was gonna taste. Never had strawberries with onions. But I figured if I could eat hog brains, I could eat this. I took a small bite of the fritter. It was delicious. I wiped the strawberry preserves from the corner of my mouth and said, "Miz Lula Maye, these strawberry-onion fritters are dyn-o-mite!"

After we finished eating, I cleaned up while Miz Lula Maye went to sit in her special chair. Her cats must have caught a whiff of the fritters. They came a runnin' and scratchin' up to the back screen door like somebody had yelled "Come and get it!"

"It's a shame they can't have any," I said in a pitiful sounding voice. But what I really thought was, I ain't sharin' any of my food with them, and I sho' ain't opening the door.

Miz Lula Maye's cats didn't need any onions, no how. They probably already got bad breath, I thought. I could brush my teeth with baking soda after I eats onions. But cats couldn't brush their teeth. Or could they? Hmmm, I wondered. Is there such a thing as toothpaste for cats? I got right tickled with myself.

While I wiped off the table, I started thinkin' up a real funny joke. What if I used Mr. Jonathan's toothbrush on one of Miz Lula Maye's cats? I laughed so hard on the inside, tears drizzled out of my eyes. That'd sure be a good way to welcome Mr. PROPER to the family!

Chapter THREE

Brown

Stuff

Out of all my foolishness, I hadn't noticed that
Miz Lula Maye had fallen asleep in her recliner. I
sat down on the couch to wait for her to wake up.

When I say *her* recliner, I mean that for real.
It's her recliner and only her recliner. Can't
nobody else but Miz Lula Maye sit in her recliner.
Why? 'Cause Jack Jr. said so. He bought it for her
as a Christmas gift last year. According to Miz
Lula Maye, when he drug it into the house he
said, "Auntie Maye, this here is yo' chair. Don't
let nobody else sit in it buts you."

I can't believe Jack Jr. had the nerve to come
up in here tellin' Miz Lula Maye what to do with

her chair. The way I see it is if you gonna give somebody a gift, they oughts to be able to do with it whatever they wants to do. If she wants to let other people sit in the stupid recliner, so be it! Besides, I personally would like to try it out for myself. It's probably the most comfortable chair in the whole entire house.

Probably the rest of Miz Lula Maye's chairs would be more comfortable, too, if she didn't have 'em all covered in that old hard, yellowed plastic. It's sharp enough to cut skin. Why do people do that?

When I get old and have my own pad, I ain't puttin' plastic over my furniture. I wants all my chairs to be soft and comfortable.

I was about to nod off myself when Miz Lula Maye hopped up so quickly I wondered if something was 'dah matter. "Come on, child," she said. "I gots something to show ya." So, I followed right behind her. Most old folks move around slow, but not Miz Lula Maye, especially after she's had a little catnap.

We ended up in Miz Lula Maye's bedroom. I hadn't spent hardly no time in her bedroom.

Most adults I know says their bedroom is off-limits to children. In other words, Keep Out! Do Not Enter! Expect a whippin' if you come in! Some people even keeps their bedroom door locked. That's strange, I thought. What could somebody have in their bedroom that would be worth keepin' the door locked?

Miz Lula Maye had several boxes on her bed. Some of the boxes looked like hatboxes. The round ones had colorful, pretty designs and flowers. Looked like they'd all been covered in wallpaper or material or something.

"Miz Lula Maye, are hats in all of these here beautiful boxes?" I asked.

"Not a one," she said. Then she pointed towards her closet saying, "That's where I keeps my hatboxes." Wow! I thought. Somebody definitely loves hats. There had to be twenty boxes on the top shelf of Miz Lula Maye's closet.

"How many hats do you have?" I asked with amazement.

"Well, Sylvia, I reckons only the Lord knows. I ain't never bothered counting."

I love plundering and going through old stuff.

I love thinking and wondering what it must've been like living a long time ago, like in the forties or fifties.

"Miz Lula Maye, what can we do first? Can we go through your hat boxes? Can we go through your boxes on the bed? Where should we start?"

I was so excited, it tickled Miz Lula Maye. "Calm down, child! Calm down!" she said laughing. "Let's see, now. It could take a right smart bit of time going through all the hatboxes in my closet. How about we saves that for another day? Will that be alright with you? Besides, I pulled these boxes out on the bed for you and Jonathan."

Hold on. I wasn't ready to do an activity or anything else with Mr. Jonathan. I barely knew him. Besides, he'd talk sixty minutes worth for every box on the bed. He'd want to make everything baby clear (like I'm a dummy), and it would take forever. I must leave, I thought. I've gotta get outta here. And fast. "Think quick, Sylvia!" I said to myself. "Think quick, now!"

Johnny-quick-on-the-spot, I developed severe, excruciating, almost life-threatening pains in my stomach. I grabbed my stomach and doubled over, practically falling to my knees. I yelled out, "Oh, no! Oh, God! It's my stomach! My stomach!" I moaned and groaned. Then I moaned and I groaned some more.

Miz Lula Maye quickly cleared an area at the foot of her bed so I could lie down. I felt awful pretending 'n all to be sick, but I wasn't ready to start trying to get close to Mr. Jonathan. To me, things like that take time and shouldn't be rushed. I wanted it to be just me and Miz Lula Maye going through the boxes together. In this case, three would definitely be a crowd.

Miz Lula Maye was so concerned about me. "Lord, I wonder if it was the fried hog brains and eggs?" she said with a puzzled look on her face. "Or maybe the onions? Onions might not agrees with you, Sylvia. Some folks can't eat onions."

Mr. Jonathan musta heard me, 'cause he came rushing in like he was a fireman coming to put out a fire. "What in heavens is going on? Did you hurt yourself, Sylvia? Should I call a doctor?" he said all in one breath.

Of course, I had to crank up my sickness. I

continued to act out the latest episode in my solo motion picture. I'm a movie star, you know. At least, in my pretend, make-believe world I am. I'm somebody strong, black, and beautiful like Pam Grier, or should I say "Foxy Brown."

Miz Lula Maye had disappeared for a minute or so. I could hear her ramblin' around in the kitchen. She returned with a glass of cold water and a spoon filled with something brown and oily lookin'.

"What's that brown stuff?" I whispered like I was near death. Whatever it was in the spoon sure smelled awful. I gagged and coughed. If my stomach wasn't sick before, it was sick after smelling that brown stuff. Mr. Jonathan standing over me like I was dead made matters double-worse.

"Why, it's my secret stomachache remedy. I even added some sugar to give it a sweeter taste," Miz Lula Maye said with a suspicious smile.

She held the spoon up to my lips. I tried keeping my mouth closed and holding my breath at the same time. It's hard to do. Actually, it's impossible, 'cause you got to breathe sometime.

Finally, Miz Lula Maye gently forced the spoon into my mouth. I swallowed that brown stuff and chased it down as quickly as I could with cold water. "Nasty! That's the nastiest stuff I've ever tasted in my whole entire life!" I said making a face that meant yucky.

"Yes, sweetie, I know," said Miz Lula Maye. "But it works in minutes. You'll be like new after sitting on the toilet. Let's see now, a girl your size, about ten minutes. It'll work your bowels through about two or three times. Then you'll feel a whole lot better."

It took a second for what she said to click. "Oh, my God, no!" I groaned. "Not a LAX-A-TIVE!" Momma had given me a laxative once before. It was the most awful, painful, and disgusting thing that's ever happened to me. I swore I'd never let it happen again.

My insides were starting to feel funny, and now I was moaning for real. Mr. Jonathan was looking at me like I'd turned into an oversized bullfrog. I looked over at him with a mean frown. I wanted to say so bad, "What you lookin' at? Get out of here!" But I didn't.

While I was rolling around on the bed moaning, "This is awful. Not a LAX-A-TIVE!" Mr. Jonathan eased his way toward the door. I heard him saying to Miz Lula Maye that he was driving to town for a spell. He told her not to bother cooking dinner, 'cause he was planning to pick up some barbecue from Pete's Pit. Normally this would sound good. But now when I thought about hot and spicy barbecue with its vinegary taste, it was too much. I grabbed my stomach and ran to the bathroom as fast as I could without falling.

I stayed in the bathroom forever. I felt like I was locked up in jail. Miz Lula Maye knocked on the door about every ten minutes or so to see if I was okay. I can't believe she tricked me like that. What in heavens was in that stuff to go through me like that, so fast 'n all? My stomach percolated like a coffeepot, and the smell—I don't even want to mention.

When it was all over, my body felt weightless, like there was nothing inside of me but bones. I stood up to wash my hands, and it almost felt like I was going to pass out. "Must of lost twenty pounds," I said to myself, looking in the mirror above the sink. I washed my hands about ten times. Then I rinsed my mouth out with cold water and washed my face.

Miz Lula Maye's bathroom only has one teeny tiny window. I raised it as high as it would go. Unfortunately, the air wasn't stirring around enough to push the funky smell out. I didn't want anybody to think I smelled that bad. I usually don't. Honest!

This was so mega-awfully embarrassing, I didn't know if I had the nerves to ever come out of the bathroom. I could see it in the *Wakeview Review:* "Ten-year-old Girl Dies on Toilet."

I cracked open the bathroom door and stuck my head out, first peeping to the right, then to the left. Lord, please don't let Jack Jr. have come over here while I was stuck on the toilet, I thought. I'll never hear the last of this most embarrassing moment in my whole entire life. I tiptoed back into Miz Lula Maye's bedroom.

I found Miz Lula Maye sitting on the bed. She was busy going through a beautiful red and green box decorated with gold jingle bells around the top. Without looking up, Miz Lula Maye said, "How you feeling? I sure hope you not mad at me. I thought ya' knew what the brown stuff was."

"No, Miz Lula Maye, I ain'ts mad at you," I said. "I just feel so weak, like I'm about to faint."

Miz Lula Maye smiled and patted my shoulders with her hands. "Well, if you faints, I'll catch ya!" she said. "Won't let my best friend fall. You gots to admit it, though. Don't you feel better? Everybody needs a good cleaning out from time to time."

Chapter FOUR

Old
Photos

Miz Lula Maye said it would be okay for me to stretch out across her bed until I felt steady again. I lay on my stomach so I could have a good look at all her stuff. This was just perfect! Mr. Jonathan was out of sight, and I had Miz Lula Maye all to myself, just the way I'd planned. Well, almost . . . minus the laxative.

Miz Lula Maye must not throw away nothing. I saw old church bulletins, newspaper clippings, birthday cards, matchbooks, wedding napkins neatly folded in half, and birthday cards.

Now, that's probably what's taking up all the

space in these hatboxes, I thought. Birthday cards. Anybody who has lived one hundred years ought to have a trillion birthday cards. And I believe that Miz Lula Maye hasn't thrown away not a one.

She also had a lot of funeral programs from family and friends she has outlived. I didn't know that I liked the look of funeral programs. "Miz Lula Maye, why do dead people's picture have to be on the front of the program?" I asked.

"Folks usually try and find a good, happy photo of their loved one so the program can be a keepsake, a good memory of when the person was alive," she told me.

I looked at her a bit strange and said, "Well, why would you want to have a keepsake of someone who is dead and gone?"

Miz Lula Maye smiled and said, "Oh, baby, it's for remembering."

"Wouldn't remembering just make you sad?" I asked.

"Well, that depends," said Miz Lula Maye.

"Depends on what?"

"Death is a part of life. Everything that lives

must die. Sometimes it depends on how close you were with the person. And sometimes it depends on how the person died or how long they suffered."

Miz Lula Maye said that she didn't want a lot of cryin' and sadness at her funeral. She wanted her homegoing to be a celebration of the happy, long life she lived. She talked like she'd already planned for her funeral. Talking about that kinda stuff felt super weird.

I quickly changed the topic after Miz Lula Maye started going into details about which songs she wanted sung at her funeral. I could hear her humming "This Little Light of Mine" as I scanned the photos on the bed.

I got to see all kinds of photos. We started with the oldest ones. They were all in black and white. I guess that's all they had back then, at least black folks. These pictures made everybody's skin look so smooth. Waves and finger waves; curls, tight curls, and pin curls; and buns must have been in style for these sistas. Cat-eye-shaped glasses were very popular. Accordin' to Miz Lula Maye, all the ladies had a pair. Miz Lula

Maye still has a pair that she wears almost all the time. She also has another pair that she sometimes wears when she gets dressed up and wants to look foxy.

"Sylvia, here is a picture of my late husband." Miz Lula Maye held up a picture that looked like an old painting. The edges were wrinkled and torn.

"What was his name?" I asked.

"Who? You talkin' 'bout this handsome fellow? His name was Matthew Abraham Maye. Everybody called him Matt for short. He was dressed in his Sunday church goin' clothes in this picture. Lord, he sho' was something sharp lookin' when he got all cleaned up." I'm not sure, but I think Miz Lula Maye was blushing.

All the while Miz Lula Maye was talking, I was lookin' at the faces of my family and trying to memorize their names. All these folks belonged on my family tree, but I didn't know where to put everybody. I knew Miz Lula Maye would help me, but I was feelin' kinda shy about askin'. I guess I ain't used to bein' part of a family bigger than two people.

Back at my house, Momma doesn't have boxes of photos like Miz Lula Maye. She does have one photo of me when I was a baby. The only other photo in our entire house is a picture of Momma and me at a beach. I'm probably around one or two years old. Don't know if I was walkin' yet or not. I was the cutest little juicy baby girl. I'm wearing a little pink outfit my momma called a romper and a bonnet that looks too big for my little head.

Momma looks about the same in this photo as she does now. She's a light-brown-skinned woman with long reddish brown hair that she always wears in one long ponytail. She's slim and kinda tall for a woman, I guess. She never wears no makeup. Zip, zap, nothing. Momma's pretty, but she always seems to have a tired, empty look on her face.

What's surprising about this photo is that Momma looks happy. I could never understand why Momma always looks so sad and tired. Well, I do know why she's tired. She works all the time. But the sad part, I wasn't sure why she looked so sad.

I might look like my momma in some ways, but I'm nothing like her. She's quiet, keeps to herself, and acts so serious. As for me, keepin' quiet is something I definitely don't do. I like to have fun and I loves to talk. Maybe I get that from Miz Lula Maye. I do believe that she likes talkin' just as much as I do.

One of Miz Lula Maye's photos stood out like an orange in a barrel of apples. It was a picture of a young boy smiling so wide it musta hurt, standing next to a big snowman. I turned the photo over and read out loud, "Jon-Jon, age ten, Christmas Eve."

Miz Lula Maye looked at the photo and started to chuckle. "Lord, I remember that day," she said. "It rarely snows around here in December, but that year it snowed on Christmas Eve. Jonathan was determined to build a snowman. He stayed outside so long, he nearly froze his fingers and toes off."

Miz Lula Maye pointed at the snowman's hat. "Somehow Jon-Jon convinced his grandpa to let him borrow his one and only work hat. Jon-Jon felt that the snowman wasn't complete unless it had a hat. His reasoning was that it might not ever snow on Christmas Eve for the rest of his life and that it was a miracle to have enough snow on Christmas Eve to even make a snowman. He had to finish what he'd started." Miz Lula Maye smiled at the memory. "Can't say any of my other childrens have ever taken a picture with a snowman on Christmas Eve."

"Miz Lula Maye, I would've been the same way," I said. "I've never built a snowman, period. I ain't never seen a white Christmas, either."

Miz Lula Maye looked at me and laughed. "Well, Miss Sylvia, don't be surprised. There's a first time for practically everything."

I examined every inch of the photo. There was something special about it. I could hardly believe this was the same Mr. Jonathan that was my dad.

"Miz Lula Maye," I said, "what should I call Mr. Jonathan? I don't know whether to call him Dad, Daddy, Pop, Pa, Papa, Father, Mr. Jonathan, just Jonathan, Jon-Jon, or what."

"Well, Sylvia," said Miz Lula Maye, "the best thing for you to do is to ask him for yourself. That way you'll hear it from the horse's mouth. That way you can't go wrong."

"Horse? Who's talkin' about a horse?" Mr. Jonathan called from the living room. Miz Lula Maye poked her head out the bedroom door and saw that he was empty-handed. "I thought you were gonna stop at Pete's Pit," she said.

"I thought so, too, but Pete's Pit was closed. The sign on the door indicated that Pete was on vacation," Mr. Jonathan said in a disappointed voice.

Miz Lula Maye headed for the kitchen to look for something to cook for dinner, and Mr. Jonathan came to see what I was doing. I held up my favorite picture of him as he entered the room.

"Oh, my goodness!" he said. "Looka here! Looka here! Boy, do I remember this one. Me and the only snowman I ever had for Christmas." Mr. Jonathan grabbed the picture from my hand as if it were a hundred dollar bill. "Sylvia, where did you get this?"

At this very moment, the expression on big Jon-Jon's face was the same as the expression on little Jon-Jon's ten-year-old face in the photo. He

stood there with the biggest grin a grown man could make and shook his head in amazement. I could see that Mr. Jonathan was not about to return my favorite photo of him no time soon. And even worse still, Mr. Jonathan had invited himself to sit a spell in Miz Lula Maye's room with me. I decided it was a good time to get going.

"Momma!" I said as I jumped to my feet. "I'd better head home. Momma will be home soon. See ya'll later!"

Miz Lula Maye had her head in the icebox when I rushed out the door. "Grandma!" Mr. Jonathan called from the bedroom. "What else do you have of me stashed away in these boxes? Where's your secret hole? I used to know. I just can't seem to remember at the moment."

A secret hole? What in tarnations is a secret hole? I wondered. I stopped on the porch steps long enough to hear Miz Lula Maye yell back, "Jonathan! Come from outta my bedroom, rights now! Don't you go to snoopin' round here lookin' for any of my secret holes. You worser than Jack Jr. wantin' to know other folks' business. Wanting to know where I keeps my privates belongins. That's for me to know and you nots to find out."

My mind began to race. Is a secret hole something outside dug down in the ground? Where is Miz Lula Maye's secret hole and what does she keep in it? Not knowing was about to kill me cold. I gotta know more about secret holes, I thought as I ran down the road toward home.

After passing Jack Jr.'s house, I could see the kitchen light on over the sink. "Shoot!" I said. I was trying to beat Momma home. I hoped she hadn't gotten into my room. I left all of my family tree stuff on my bed right out in the open. Momma wouldn't be happy about that.

"Hey, girl. What you been up to all day?" Momma asked as I came in the door.

"I ain't been up to nothin' much," I said. "Just hanging out with Miz Lula Maye."

As fast as I could, I went to my bedroom, gathered up all the family tree papers, and stuck them under my bed. Then I walked back out to the kitchen, trying to act real cool.

"So, have you had supper?" Momma asked.

"Not yet, but I'm not really hungry, at least not right now."

"Good, that will give me enough time to cook a pot of succotash. Jack Jr. left us a basket full of fresh okra, tomatoes, and sweet corn at the back door. Wasn't that nice of him?" said Momma with a little smile.

I sat down at the kitchen table and watched

while Momma turned on the water and washed four ears of corn at the sink. Then she rambled through a drawer to find a knife. It was so quiet that everything she did seemed twice as loud as normal.

Zzzip, zzzip, zzzip went the knife as Momma shaved the corn from its cob.

"Did you see Jonathan?" Momma asked without looking at me. She dumped the kernels into a tall pot on the stove.

"Yep," I said.

Thunk, thunk, thunk. Momma cut up okra on the kitchen counter. Then she added some butter beans from the freezer to the pot. "What did you talk about?" she asked.

"Didn't talk much with him today," I told her. "I stayed with Miz Lula Maye while he went into town for barbecue from Pete's Pit."

"So you didn't talk about anything?" asked Momma, finally looking up at me.

The nerve of her. I couldn't believe it, but my momma had the nerve to be full of questions. Should I act like I'm crazy and ignore the woman and not answer one of her questions? Or should I do what's right and answer her? I thought about it really hard before opening my mouth.

"He said Pete's Pit was closed. I guess Pete's on vacation," I explained. That ought to be good enough, I agreed with myself. Tell her only what I want her to know.

As usual, Momma and I didn't talk much for the rest of the night. "Humph," I said with attitude when I was getting ready for bed. That was okay with me. All I could do was think about secret holes. I knew I had to ask questions about them. I had to know the details. I wouldn't be Sylvia Freeman if I didn't.

Chapter  FIVE

Sharing Secrets

The next morning when I dashed out the back door, I spotted you-know-who walking down Pearle Road. I hid behind the trash barrel and watched Mr. Jonathan as he headed in my direction. What if he was coming to visit? That would not be a good thing.

"Praise the Lord," I whispered as he walked over to the Juke Joint. He was probably going to get all nosy up in Jack Jr.'s business.

I took off running for Miz Lula Maye's as fast as I could. When I popped up at Miz Lula Maye's screen door breathing heavy, she looked worried. "What's the matter, Sylvia? Is something wrong, baby? You seen a snake?" she asked.

I was nervous about asking, but I had to know. "Miz Lula Maye," I gasped, "what's a secret hole? I heard Mr. Jonathan ask you yesterday and I know you said that it was private but I can't help it. I gotta know."

Miz Lula Maye laughed. "Sylvia, baby, sit down and catch your breath and I'll tell you about secret holes."

Boy, oh, boy! I sho' got Miz Lula Maye talking. "Secret holes was hiding places," she said. "Long ago, when I first got married, folks had secret holes hidden in places all throughout their house to keep important papers. Most folks kept birth certificates and papers about their land and their house. Money was the biggest thing folks kept in their secret holes. That's mainly why it had to be kept a secret."

"So people held on to their own money?" I asked. "What if the house burned down?"

"If there was gonna be a fire, more than likely it was gonna be in the kitchen," explained Miz Lula Maye. "Folks never kept a secret hole in the kitchen. Secret holes were usually near the front of the house, hidden in places you'd never think of. Nowadays, things have changed. People have safes now, and folks keep their money in the bank. As for me, I keeps a little stash hidden in the house for emergencies."

Now she really had every ounce of my attention. "Miz Lula Maye, you mean you still have a secret hole?" I asked, looking around for clues. "Where? Tell me. Please? Where's some good hiding places? Miz Lula Maye, where's your secret hole?"

Miz Lula Maye put her finger up to her mouth and said, "Shhhh." Then she motioned "follow me." And of course, I followed.

She asked me to help her pull her bed out from against the wall. I was so excited, I think I could've moved it all by myself. We pulled the bed out just far enough for us to squeeze our bodies behind the headboard. I began rubbing my hands over the wall to see if I could feel something. I looked up at Miz Lula Maye, and she shook her head and smiled. I felt like we were playing some kinda hide-'n-go-seek game. Next I rubbed the wooden slats on the floor. Probably

looked like some half-blind person looking for lost eyeglasses. I looked up at Miz Lula Maye a second time. "Shoot! That's not it, either?"

Miz Lula Maye laughed. Then she nudged my shoulder for me to move over. Lo and behold, to my surprise, Miz Lula Maye's secret hole wasn't in the wall and wasn't in the floor. Her secret hole was in one of the posts attached to the headboard of her bed. Down at the bottom of the post was a fancy knob shaped like a box. There was a tiny piece of fishing line hanging from the corner of the box. Miz Lula Maye yanked at the line just the right way, and POOF! the door popped open.

"Wow!" I said. "This is Double-O-Seven typa stuff. This is B-A-D, Miz Lula Maye!"

In this particular secret hole, Miz Lula Maye had her children's school records and birth certificates. "Do you have your birth certificate hidden in one of your secret holes?" I asked.

Miz Lula Maye shook her head. "I don't have a copy of my birth certificate. I really don't know if I ever had one in the first place."

Her mother had her in a house, not a hospital. The house Miz Lula Maye was born in burned to the ground when she was a baby. "Probably set to fire on purpose," said Miz Lula Maye in a sad sounding voice. "I came along during a time when the devil was busy burning up folks' houses, trying to run them out of town or back to Africa."

When her house burned, all the birthing records burned, too. So that was the end of that. "How do you know when it's time for your birthday?" I asked.

"Well, Sylvia, to tells you the honest-to-goodness truth, I don't," she said. "I don't know exactly, but I feels like I'm pretty close." Miz Lula Maye thinks she was born way, way back in 1878. But who knows? She may actually be older than one hundred!

"When I was young, folks didn't really celebrate birthdays every year like the way people do now," she said. "Age wasn't as important as a person's ability to do certain chores. My mother died when I was around your age, Sylvia. I was the oldest of three, so I ended up raising my brother and sister. I also did the cooking and the cleaning and the sewing."

Miz Lula Maye says she never really thought

about how old she was until she was asked to be married. "Matt wanted to know how old I was before he went to my papa to ask for my hand in marriage. I told him that I thought I was around fifteen or sixteen. He wanted to know which one. Was I fifteen or was I sixteen? I told him I really didn't know. When he asked my papa about my age, well, Papa definitely didn't know how old I was. Anyhow, he married me just the same."

These secret holes sure brought back ancient memories for Miz Lula Maye. We were both very still for a while. Then to change up the quiet mood, I asked, "Do you have any more secret holes, Miz Lula Maye?"

"Let's see. It's been years, child, since I been up in these holes," Miz Lula Maye said. She opened the other secret hole at the bottom of the bedpost. A piece of paper folded in a square was stuffed inside. The paper had yellowed to a golden brownish color, especially along the folds. You could tell it probably had not been unfolded in years and years.

When Miz Lula Maye opened up the paper, I could see that it was a map. There was a road shaped like the letter Y and lots of fields. On the road were four houses. "Man, this is a nice drawing," I said. "What's it supposed to be?"

"Don't you recognize it, Sylvia?" said Miz Lula Maye with a ca-cacka-cacka-cacka-sounding laugh. She pointed at the map. "That's my house. The one we's in right now. It's old as dirt."

Miz Lula Maye's told me about how her husband, my great-grandpa, inherited the acres of land and houses from a white man named Coleman. My great-grandpa's dad had put himself in an early grave working for the Coleman family. When he died, I reckons they felt partly the blame. So when the landowner, old man Coleman, passed away, it was printed in his will that the land be given to the family of Miz Lula Maye's husband.

Folks couldn't believe it. A white man left a black man not only his land, but houses, animals, and timber. "Folks always said old man Coleman went crazy before he died," said Miz Lula Maye. "Praise God, anyhow! Crazy or not, it sho' was a blessing."

I spent a long time looking at the map.

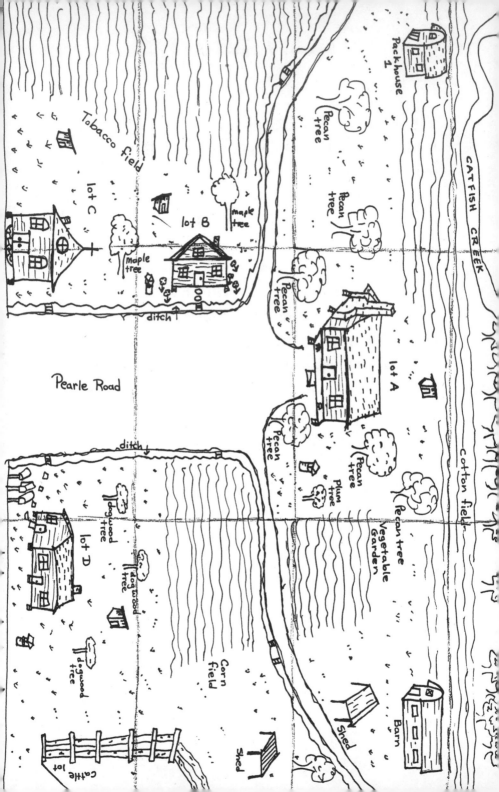

I couldn't believe I didn't recognize Pearle Road right away. It was unbelievable, but almost everything on that old map was exactly the same as it is now. The biggest difference was that back when the map was made, Jack Jr.'s Juke Joint was a church. I found my house across from the church and Jack Jr.'s house next to Miz Lula Maye's, which was at the end of the road.

I rubbed my finger over Miz Lula Maye's house. "Did you draw this map, Miz Lula Maye?" I asked. She smiled, "Well, yes, I reckons I did draw it."

Suddenly, I knew it was time to take the plunge. "I'm workin' on a drawing, too. I'm tryin' to draw my family tree."

Miz Lula Maye's eyes sparkled like stars. "You are? Oh, Sylvia, that's a great idea! You so smart, I don't know what I'm gonna do with ya."

I smiled, holding my head down. "I'm not that smart. I can't get it right. I don't know who or where to put folks."

"You just ask me," said Miz Lula Maye. "I'll try and remember as much as I can to help you, baby."

It was as easy as that. I couldn't believe it. I'm

just not used to getting my questions answered.

The front screen door slammed, and Miz Lula Maye and me jumped like we had been caught doin' something. I quickly folded the map back the way it was, and Miz Lula Maye placed it back in the secret hole and closed the door.

"Where are the two most beautiful ladies in Wakeview hiding?" Mr. Jonathan called out. We must have had sneaky looks on our faces when we came into the living room, but Mr. Jonathan didn't notice. He was already runnin' his mouth.

"Nanna Maye, that Jack Jr. is some character. Did you know that he is courting some girl who already has another boyfriend? The girl is already spoken for. She's been DJ Hot's girlfriend for a long time, and Jack's known it. She is just using him. I tried to tell him. She thinks since he runs the Juke Joint that he has a lot of money. Well, from the looks of things around here, I'd have to say she's not too sharp. I don't think Jack is rolling around in anything valuable, let alone money."

Uh-oh. I could see by Miz Lula Maye's face that Mr. Jonathan had gone too far. One thing I've learned about Miz Lula Maye is that she protects the people she loves. When you make a mistake, she'll fuss you out and set you straight, but just let somebody else try to do it to one of her own.

"Jon-Jon Jonathan Bernard Maye, don't you come up in here bad-mouthin' Jack Jr.!" Here it comes! This was gonna be quite a show.

And now, over in this corner, wearing a blue dress with white flowers and pink house shoes, weighing in at one hundred and thirty pounds, not defeated, the incredible, irresistible, one-hundred-year-old feather-weight champion of the world, Miz Lu . . . la . . . Maye!!!

Next, in this corner, wearing khaki shorts, a white T-shirt with sleeves rolled up, brown leather sandals with dusty, crusty, ashy big feet, weighing in at two hundred pounds (maybe?), TKO unknown, it's the daddy from the dead, champion of surprises, Mr. Jon . . . Jon . . . Jon..a..than Maye!!!

Now, let's shake hands and fight a clean fight. Ring! Ring! Ring! Let's get ready to rum . . . ble!

I settled in to watch, 'cause I knew that Mr. Jonathan was about to be set straight. I had the best seat in the house.

SIX

Storm Comin'

After Miz Lula Maye showed me her secret holes, I got to thinking. That night, I lay in bed and wondered if Momma had a secret hole. I knew it was no use asking. If I started to talkin' about secrets and holes, she might get some ideas. She might go and empty hers so I would remain clueless and in the dark. If I was ever gonna find out anything about Momma, I was gonna have to go a different path. I had to find out if Momma had a secret hole, and I had to know what was in it.

When I woke up the next morning at about 5:30, Momma was getting ready for work. The sky was pure white. Lord, I sure hope it doesn't rain, I thought. I have plans to make and work to do. And I can't do either if it rains. If it rains, Momma can't work in the fields. If Momma is home, I can't search for secret holes. I can't search for clues or answers.

I could hear a heavy thunder roaring. But it wasn't a storm. It was the wheels on the morning train rolling on those rusty tracks across the road. Then I could hear the whistle as the train approached.

Whistling and roaring. Whistling and roaring. Whistling and roaring. It got closer and closer and louder and louder. The train driver laid down real hard on the horn as it crossed over the highway. Then the sound of the whistling and roaring got weak. Then weaker and weaker. Then it got far away. Then farther and farther away, as it traveled on to the next town.

In a way—even though it wasn't a storm—in a way, the sound of a train reminds me of a storm. When a storm comes, you can hear it coming from a distance. It gets close, then closer, and then it finally arrives. Then, when it passes, it gets far, then farther and farther away, until it's completely gone. Things get quiet and calm again. So a storm and a train are kinda like different, but the same. They both make a lot of noise. Shake things up a bit coming and going. Passing all over the land with a roar.

All that thinkin' about trains and storms put me back to sleep for an hour or so. When I woke up, Momma was gone. I knew I had to move fast if a storm was coming. I washed my face and brushed my teeth so I wouldn't have dragon breath.

I took a flash glance at my hair in the mirror. "Forget it! Darling, you don't have time to comb your hair today," said the mirror. I grabbed the first pair of shorts I found in the drawer and a top. They didn't really match, but that didn't matter to me today.

I figured the first place I should search for secret holes was in Momma's bedroom. That's probably where she's got everything hidden, I thought. I needed to think like a robber. If I was a robber, what would I do? Where would I search? Sometimes robbers (at least the ones on

TV) have a map. That's it! I realized. That's what I needed to do, draw a map so nothing would be overlooked. I had to pay attention to the tiniest details.

I sat in the doorway and drew a map of my momma's bedroom. First I drew a big square. It took up the entire space on my paper. Next I added the doors and the windows and all of the

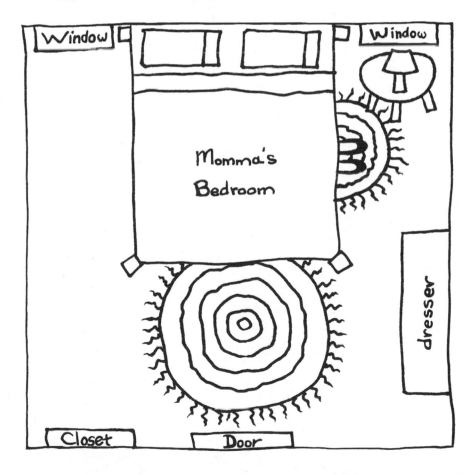

furniture. I drew the rug in the middle of the room with the fringes all around the edges and the half-circle rug on the right side of Momma's bed where she leaves her house shoes. Detail is important, I reminded myself, so I even drew the house shoes.

Then I was ready to search. Momma's bed doesn't have bedposts like Miz Lula Maye's, so that was out from the start. But I did search the back of Momma's headboard. No secret holes. After looking under the nightstand table, I crawled under the bed with a flashlight. Spiderwebs got all in my hair, and dust got all over my clothes. No secret holes under the bed, either. Just some old shoe boxes. Momma keeps her good shoes in shoe boxes to keep the dust off 'em.

The dresser was too heavy for me to push out from the wall, so I aimed the flashlight just right to see if there were any secret holes hidden behind it. Nothing! It's a shame I don't have an older brother or sister. One sure would've come in handy right about then. Someone stronger and bigger could've helped push and move dressers and beds. Unfortunately, I had no one I could call on for help—mostly because what I was doing was top secret. It was between me, myself, and I.

It must have taken an hour for me to go through the closet. First I had to pull out all of Momma's unpacked boxes before I could search the walls inside the closet. Then I took a look inside the boxes. I even searched the closet floor, but nothing.

The last place I could think of to search in Momma's bedroom was under the rugs. The only thing I found under both rugs was dirt, two safety pins, several strands of hair, and one bobby pin. I had run out of places to look. Either this room had no secret holes or I was just too stupid to find the darn things. I was really starting to lose hope. But then I heard Miz Lula Maye's voice in my head: "All hope is never lost."

I decided it was time to take a break and do some thinking. I made a peanut butter and jelly sandwich and some grape Kool-Aid for lunch. All of a sudden, the daylight disappeared. I ran to look out the window over the kitchen sink. A humongous dark cloud covered the sky. The wind had definitely picked up. A ball of dust blew around on Pearle Road like a baby twister. The storm that had been brewin' all day was on its way. It was probably in the next town. I was running out of time.

I ate fast and studied the map some more. Turning the map right side up, then upside down, I checked for things I might have missed. It was a pretty good map, if I do say so myself. I liked the way I drew the fringe on the rug and Momma's cute little house shoes.

Suddenly, while I was looking at my drawing of the house shoes, an object popped into my head. A shoe box. "Why a shoe box?" I said out loud.

There were three shoe boxes under Momma's bed. I hadn't bothered to look in them because I knew that was where Momma kept her good shoes. Except Momma only had two pairs of good shoes.

I dropped my sandwich and ran to Momma's bedroom. I was so anxious, I felt lightheaded and dizzy.

It was still there, right where I last saw it under

the bed. The mysterious third shoe box. It looked a lot older than the other ones. I quickly slid the shoe box out from under the bed and went into my room and locked the door.

First I sat on my bed, but it wasn't comfortable. So I slid down to the floor and sat cross-legged with the shoe box resting on my legs. I was so nervous, my hands wouldn't let me open the shoe box. I just sat there, not knowing what to do. I gazed at the top of the box. Then I looked at the shoe size and the price tag. This really must be an old shoe box, I thought, 'cause it's hard to find a pair of shoes under eight dollars nowadays (especially Sunday shoes).

The wind was really picking up outside. It had begun to rain, and the thunder and lightning was approaching quickly. I knew Momma would be walking through the door any minute. Holding my breath and shaking like a rattlesnake, I lifted the top off the shoe box and discovered a stack of letters. They were all addressed to Momma and the return address on the envelopes said Chicago, Illinois.

Now that I had actually found something, I

started to feel guilty. Going through Momma's private things was not right. There ain't no two ways about it. Should I be so bad? I asked myself. Should I honestly read a letter that's not mine? Or should I just put back the shoe box and forget all about this nonsense?

Something inside of me, deep inside of my heart and mind, was telling me to read at least one of those letters. BOOM! BOOM! BOOM! Thunder crashed outside. That was a sign. I knew it was. That was God telling me to follow my heart.

"Okay, God!" I said.

I picked up the first letter. The envelope was a very pretty lavender and the letter sheets matched the envelope. "Dear Sis," I read out loud. "Oh, my Lord!" I said shaking my head. "Momma's not an only child! Momma has a sister! All this time, I just knew there was somebody else. I just knew it!"

I kept reading. At first, I read so fast I couldn't make heads or tails out of the letter. There was something about a baby. I tried to slow down and read the whole thing from start to finish.

Oct. 29, 1967

Dear Sis,

How's my baby? I can't believe she's already a month old. I miss you both. Real bad. So bad it's got me believing in God (can you believe that) and praying all day and all night. I keep praying to God asking whether or not I or we did the right thing.

I know you are the best mother my baby girl could ever have. She's going to have a better childhood than we did. That's what's important. Don't waste your pretty little head on me worrying about stuff. I'm going to get strong enough to sing again. I know it. Ain't that good news?

Well kiss baby girl for me and you take care of yourself.

Love Ya!

Sherry Marie

When I finished the letter, my mouth was dry and my whole body was tremblin' like I'd been standin' in a freezer. I looked at the date at the top of the letter. October 29, 1967. My birthday was September 29, 1967. "Wait a minute Wait just one minute!" I yelled, jumping to my feet. Was . . . could I be the baby?

I searched the end of the letter again to read the name signed there. "This Sherry Marie person is my real momma?" I questioned the letter. What kind of momma would give away her baby? And why? I looked at the letter again. So she could get strong enough to sing? "I don't even believe this," I said, pacing the floor.

I threw the letter on the floor and stomped all over it with my sweaty, bare feet. I stomped so hard til my feet stung as if I was walking on the back of a porcupine. Then I stretched out on my belly. "My own, my own real mother didn't want me," I whispered to the floor. And I cried and cried and cried.

SEVEN

Seafood

Disaster

The back door slammed shut, jolting me awake. I had no idea how long I'd been asleep. "Oh, no!" I whispered. The letter stuck to the side of my face as I lifted my head up off the floor to make sure I heard what I thought I'd heard.

Momma would be madder than I could ever imagine if she knew what I'd done. And what I knew. She'd probably be mad at me for the rest of my life. I had to get myself together before she came to my room.

"Think quick, Sylvia!" I told myself. "Hide the letter!"

I slid the shoe box under my bed. Then I

folded the damp letter as small as I could. I looked frantically around my room. Where? Where should I hide it? I needed to find myself a secret hole. Finally, I picked up the lamp on the nightstand beside my bed and pushed the letter just slightly into the bottom of its base.

Everybody's got a secret, huh? I thought. Well, I can have one, too. Folks around here thinks they smart. Well, I can be smart, too!

I looked awful. I knew I did without even looking in a mirror. I tried to clean up my face. Then I fussed around my room, pacing until I could look normal. I chanted to myself, "I can stay cool. I can stay cool. I think I can stay cool. I hope and pray I can keep cool."

When I was ready, I very quietly unlocked my bedroom door. "Won't a soul know what's happened. Well, maybe God. This secret is between me and God," I told myself as I walked into the kitchen to greet Momma.

"Hey, what's up?" I tried to sound cheerful. The rain, thunder, and lightning had stopped. Peeping through the blinds in the kitchen I said, "Momma, ain't this some crazy weather here in

Wakeview? It was just fussin' up a storm, and now the sun is coming back out."

"Yeah, sho' is," Momma said as if she had a million things on her mind.

It looked like I didn't have to worry about Momma seeing I was upset. It seemed like she barely knew I was there. I was surprised to see it was almost five o'clock.

"What took you so long?" I asked. "I expected you home as soon as it started raining."

"Stopped by Miz Lula Maye's before coming in." Momma walked over to the mail basket and began looking through some bills.

Oh no! I thought. I forgot to get the mail! But Momma didn't even notice. Thank God! She didn't even know it, but she was looking at yesterday's mail.

She seemed a bit different, almost strange. And what in tarnations was she doing stopping by Miz Lula Maye's? I wondered. She wasn't the visiting type. Momma rarely stopped by anywhere. And she most definitely hadn't seemed interested in talking to Mr. Jonathan since he showed up from the dead. I didn't know why (all of a sudden) she'd decided to talk to him now.

But wait a minute, I considered. Was Momma and Mr. Jonathan girlfriend and boyfriend? Or was Mr. Jonathan and this Sherry lady boyfriend and girlfriend? So does this make Mr. Jonathan my daddy or not? Lord knows this puzzle was getting more and more harder to piece together. I felt like I was drifting back in Sylvia's World of Confusion.

We both recognized the sound of a car pulling up in the yard. Momma slowly walked to the back door and just stood there in silence. "Who is it, Momma?" I asked.

Without turning around she said, "It's Jonathan." Before I could make it over to the door, Mr. Jonathan was on the other side of the screen. They just stood there looking at each other, face to face in silence.

I heard a car door slam. Wouldn't ya know who it was? Yes, Jack Jr. "What's the hold up?" he said, grinning as he came up behind Mr. Jonathan. I tell ya, Jack Jr. has got to be the happiest person in Wakeview. And the craziest, too.

"Come on, ya'll! Auntie Maye is waiting in

the car and I'm starving," complained Jack Jr., rubbing his belly.

"Where ya'll headed?" Momma asked.

Finally Mr. Jonathan spoke. "We thought we'd all go out to eat at the Seafood Shack."

I hadn't been out to eat at a restaurant in ages, and anything sounded better than sittin' around the quiet house with Momma, trying to keep my secrets. I looked at Momma. "Momma, please say yes," I begged. "Can we go? I want us all to go."

Momma actually cracked a bit of a smile and said, "Well, I could have a taste for some shrimps. Go on then and clean yourself up so we can go."

By the time we made it to the Seafood Shack, the parking lot was packed with cars. The air smelled like something good. According to Miz Lula Maye, this place cooks with special herbs and spices. Plus, she says, they use separate fryers to fry their seafood. That way, shrimp don't taste like fish and fries don't taste like seafood.

That's all we talked about in the car on the way to the Seafood Shack. That's also all we talked about in the restaurant. It was kinda like nobody could think of anything better or safe to discuss other than seafood. Even Jack Jr. was at a loss for something different to talk about except seafood and his aching, empty belly.

Everything we ate at the Seafood Shack came in a red plastic basket shaped like a boat. The bottom of the basket was layered with white paper napkins to soak up the grease. After we ate our seafood (which, by the way, was delicious), it was like there was nothing else to do or say.

When the waitress came over to bring us our bill, I noticed her name badge. It said Sherry. My teeth almost fell out of my mouth. I couldn't believe what my eyes saw. It was like a sign. It was like something (probably the devil) was trying to get me to tell my secret. Had Momma seen the name? I wondered, trying not to panic. Could she tell that I knew it meant something? I felt like the waitress's name badge was blinking S-H-E-R-R-Y in big lit-up letters.

The only person who seemed to notice there was something wrong with me was Miz Lula Maye. When she looked at me, I knew she was trying to help. It was almost like she was using sign language with her smile and eyes. The only

problem was, I didn't really know if she knew
what she was helping me out with.

Miz Lula Maye turned and asked the waitress,
"So, what's for dessert? Do ya'll have any banana
puddin' or coconut creme pie?" The waitress left
for a moment and returned with a dessert menu.
Miz Lula Maye leaned forward and asked if I'd

like to share a piece of carrot cake with her. I agreed, even though my stomach was so nervous I didn't think it could take any more food.

Jack Jr. ordered a piece of hot apple pie with a huge scoop of vanilla ice cream sittin' on top. I thought I was going to get sick watching him sop up melted ice cream mixed with cooked apples.

I messed over my piece of cake. I ate the frosting and that's about it. The silence at our table was deadly. To take my mind off the terror, I decided to stuff myself silly and finish my cake. Then I drank every bit of my iced tea. All of a sudden, I didn't feel too good. I got up from the table and headed to the bathroom without saying a word. Halfway there, my stomach began to knot up. Everything I'd eaten was in a tug-of-war with my nerves. Shrimp, hush puppies, coleslaw, carrot cake, and iced tea was moving around in my stomach like clothes on a spin cycle in the washing machine.

If I took another step, I knew everything inside of me was gonna come up and out. I was hot and dizzy. I was sweating like I don't know what. So I stopped and tried to breathe. It worked for a second or two, then my body went into overdrive. My heart pumped as fast as it could. The restaurant began spinning around and around. I couldn't breathe. I couldn't swallow. I felt like I was choking.

Like a rocket, I let it go. I let it all go. Right on the floor in front of the bathroom door, in the restaurant. In front of everybody eating, I let it go. I tried to grab it with my hands, but there was no use. It was too much throw up for me to hold in my hands.

Some of my disgusting dinner also ended up on the bathroom door. I was so embarrassed! My hands would smell like throw up forever. Thank God, nothing got on my clothes.

Miz Lula Maye and Momma came running over. I closed my eyes and pretended to be dead in their arms. I couldn't bear to see the look on the faces of those ladies coming out the bathroom, stepping over my throw up.

I made a lot of people lose their appetites. Some people just got up and left. I felt so bad. I didn't know why it happened. Everything I ate seemed to taste fresh. I heard Miz Lula Maye say,

"One bad shrimp can make you sicker than a dog."

When I decided to open my eyes, the three of us were inside a smelly bathroom. It smelled like some other folks might've gotten sick that night, too. The smell made me gag. But nothing else came out. I don't think anything else was left inside me. Especially since the brown stuff Miz Lula Maye gave me had already cleaned me out. If I'm not careful, I thought, there ain't gonna be nothing left of me.

"You alright?" Miz Lula Maye asked while I was washing my hands. I looked up and stared directly into her eyes. Then I held my head down as if I was shame of something.

"Sylvia, childs, you can't keep things bottled up inside you. It'll make you sick. Is that why you's sick tonight?" Miz Lula Maye asked.

"Maybe," I whispered. Then I looked up at my momma, but I couldn't look her in the eyes. I just couldn't do it.

"What is it, Sylvia?" asked Miz Lula Maye.

"Sherry," I said. "The name badge . . . the waitress's name was Sherry."

I thought I saw smoke coming from my momma's nose. Yes, she's mad, I thought. I don't know why she's mad. I'm the one who ought to be mad with smoke coming out my nose. I'm the one who has been tried and lied til I nearly died.

"What's that supposed to mean?" she said. "Out with it, Sylvia! Rights now!" But I couldn't answer Momma. I covered my face with my smelly hands and just shook my head.

There was shouting and knocking going on. The shouting came from my momma and the knocking came from Mr. Jonathan and Jack Jr. They wanted to know if I was okay. Miz Lula Maye answered, "We'll be out in a minute. Go get the car and pull it up to the door."

I didn't want to leave. I knew when I got home, I'd have to answer to Momma. So I tried to make myself sick again. I even snuck and stuck my middle finger down my throat. I even tried to smell the stinky stench in the bathroom to see if it would make me sick again. Nothing worked. The only thing I could get to come out of me was tears of terror. My thoughts raced. Should I confess what I did today? Do they already know? Should I tell the truth about the letter? Should I?

Mr. Jonathan knocked on the door again. That was quick, I thought. "Oh Lord," I whispered. "If you can hear me, I needs your help. I needs your help right now!"

EIGHT

The Whole Truth

Miz Lula Maye wet a paper towel with cold water and placed it on my forehead. We all walked slowly to the car as if I was just being released from the hospital.

Mr. Jonathan opened his door and jumped out of the car to help. I looked at the car door, opened 'n all, but I couldn't move forward. I didn't want to get in the car. I swallowed whatever spit was sitting inside my dry, trembling mouth. Then I lost it.

"I want the whole truth!" I yelled as loud as I could. "And I want it right now! Right here!

Right now! And I mean it!" Yes, I said all of that, waving my right hand in the air at my folks. It was amazing. All of a sudden, I no longer felt weak.

Momma grabbed me by my arm and shoved me to a sitting position on the hood of the car. "Sit right here and don't move!" she said. Momma and Mr. Jonathan walked around to the back of the car and began arguing in a whisper. Yes, arguing in a whisper. Now, how many normal people on this here earth can actually argue and whisper in the same breath? Lord, Jesus, these here are some strange times.

Miz Lula Maye was standing in front of the car with her hands placed on her hips, observing everything. I could tell she was upset, too. But why was she upset? And who was she upset with? Miz Lula Maye wasn't too happy with me the last time I cut a fit. And now I'd done it again. I sure do know how to mess things up. Now Miz Lula Maye was probably gonna be my great-grandma and not my best friend anymore, for good this time.

I lowered my head so I wouldn't have to see

the look on Miz Lula Maye's face. But then, lo and behold, that's when the Lord finally stepped in to help. Miz Lula Maye blew up, but it wasn't at me.

"We ain't leavin' this here parking lot til you two can help keep this child from going cuckoo!" yelled Miz Lula Maye in a voice that said she meant every word.

Praise the Lord! I blew a sigh of relief and even caught myself getting ready to smile, but now was not a good time to be smiling. Boy, oh boy, Miz Lula Maye was madder now than she was that time she thought Jack Jr. had gotten rid of her cats. She marched to the back of the car and stood in front of Momma and Mr. Jonathan. I stayed put. But I did turn around so I could see Miz Lula Maye chew them out.

I couldn't quite make out what anybody was saying, but I could clearly see that Mr. Jonathan was very upset. He paced to the left, then to the right, then stopped and shook his head. Then he threw his hands up into the air and gazed at the sky, holding his hands like he was going to say his bedtime prayers. My momma just stood still in

one spot with her arms crossed over her chest. I couldn't tell for sure because Momma was holding her head down, but I think she was crying.

Finally, Miz Lula Maye came over to me and put her arm around my shoulders like she was protecting me. Even though I was in the middle of Family Terror Part 2, I felt true love from my best friend and great-grandma. "Everything's gonna be alright, baby," she said. "Now you go over there and talk to your momma."

When I walked over to Momma, we both gazed at each other as if we were meeting face to face for the first time. "Did you find the letters?" she asked very quietly.

At first, I didn't know whether to tell the truth or not. I looked at Miz Lula Maye and she gave me a nod. "Yes," I answered. It was hard, but I looked directly at my momma. I didn't want to miss a bit of what she was about to say next. Momma nodded her head up and down with her lips pressed real tight against her teeth.

"Then you know I'm not your real momma?" She paused and lowered her head like this was the hardest thing she'd ever had to say. "Your real momma is my twin sister, Sherry Marie." Tears drizzled down Momma's face and dropped like rain off her chin down onto her chest.

Miz Lula Maye came over and held Momma's hands in her hands. In a comforting voice, Miz Lula Maye told Momma, "Marie, you's a strong woman. Take as long as you need. It's time to tell her everything. Don't feel rushed. We'll be waitin' for ya back in the car." Then Miz Lula Maye left us alone.

"Sylvia," said Momma, "me and Sherry grew up in a children's home in Florida after our parents died. When we turned eighteen, we had to be out on our own." She shook her head like those musta been some hard times.

"Sherry got a job singing with a quartet up in Chicago. There was another Sherry in the group, so she started calling herself by her middle name, Marie. That's when she met Jonathan. But just when their courting got serious, Jonathan had to go to Vietnam."

Momma wiped her eyes and continued. "By the time Sherry found out that she was pregnant, Jonathan was gone. She wanted to tell your dad the truth. Lord knows, she did. But she didn't know how he would take it."

I interrupted Momma's talkin'. "So both my momma and my daddy didn't want me?" I asked.

Momma looked puzzled. "What do you mean?"

"I read the letter," I told her. "I know my real momma gave me up so she could sing."

Momma shook her head. "No, Sylvia! It wasn't like that. Girl, your momma, my sister, loved you with all of her might. If she could've changed things, she would've. I know she would've. But sometimes things happen in your life that you can't change. All you can do is make do the best you can with whats you got."

Then Momma reached out for my hands like we were about to pray or something. Believe me when I say that this was a rare moment. It was so weird, goose bumps popped up all over my arms and legs. "Sylvia, my Sherry was sick since before you was born. After she found out she was havin' you, she also found out she had cancer."

I frowned in total confusion. "Cancer? What do you mean? What are you trying to say?"

Momma began pacing back and forth in front

of me. "Sherry had to undergo her cancer treatments right after you was born. I came up from Florida to help out, and we did a lot of talking. Sherry was way too sick to take care of a brand-new baby. She, I mean, we ... we decided together that it would be best for me to take you back to Florida with me, at least until she got better.

"We didn't want you to end up in no children's home, so we thought it would be best if people thought I was your real momma. Because Marie is also my middle name, it was easy enough to start calling myself Marie Freeman instead of Terry Freeman. I moved around all the time in Florida, so there was nobody to pay attention when I came back with a different name and a new baby."

I was trying to keep everything straight. "So your real name is Terry?" I asked.

Momma nodded. "Terry Marie."

I shook my head in wonder. "So I guess I got two mommas, Momma Terry and Momma Sherry."

Momma smiled a sad smile. "Well, I guess you

could say that, in a way." She paused for a minute. Then she kinda looked like she was having an asthma attack, except Momma didn't have asthma. A whole new river of tears fell from Momma's eyes. She could barely catch her breath, let alone talk.

"Momma, what is it?" I asked.

She sniffed long and deep and cried, "Sylvia, I'm sorry. I'm as sorry as I can be, but Sherry was very sick. Cancer just wouldn't let her be. Sylvia, she died before your second birthday."

I frowned with my mouth wide open. I wasn't ready for what my ears heard. "She what? She died? My real momma is dead? That can't be! I ain't never"—Momma grabbed a hold of me and held me real tight without giving me a chance to finish what I'd planned to say.

Miz Lula Maye says the truth's a hurtin' thing. She's right. I was hurtin'. It felt like someone had knocked the wind right outta me. I just found out about my real mother and now she was dead. Been dead for years. But it was plain to see that this was hurting Momma more than it was hurting me.

Momma said that for years it was a piece of cake. It was easy pretending to be my real momma. I was just an arm baby and couldn't talk or ask questions. And that's when it became easy for her name to be just Marie.

"Your growing up has made it more difficult than I ever imagined," she said. "You're so smart, I just couldn't keep on pretending and lying to you. It came to the point that I'd just as soon keep quiet than to add one more lie to the endless pit."

I paced a few times not knowing whether to stay or walk away. "Why didn't you just tell me the truth?"

"I guess I thought if I told you I wasn't your real momma I would lose you," she said. "Maybe not now, but someday. I can't lose you. You're all I've got. If you're mad at me, well, I don't blame ya."

I grabbed my momma and gave her a big bear hug. "I love you with all my heart and soul," she said as she hugged me back.

The insides of my body wanted to explode. Is there any such thing as being too full of the truth? One side of me wanted to feel sad because Momma Sherry was dead. The other side of me wanted to feel happy because both my mommas loved me.

Jack Jr. rolled down the car window and stuck his head out. "Can we go home now?" he yelled like a three year old. We all laughed. It doesn't take much for Jack Jr. to make you laugh. There's just something about him and the silly looks on his face that makes you wanna laugh.

The ride home was a quiet one. "Are you okay, baby?" asked Miz Lula Maye squeezing my hand. I didn't answer because I didn't have an answer. I laid my head on her shoulder for most of the ride. Then I laid my head on Momma's shoulder to ask her a private question.

"Momma, do they know who you are?" I whispered in her ear. She didn't say a word. Instead, she nodded her head yes.

When Jack Jr. stopped the car at my house, we all sat there for a few minutes. It felt like everyone was looking at me, waiting for me to say something. For the first time, I didn't have nothing to say. So I got out of the car. Sticking his head out of the passenger window, Mr. Jonathan said, "Are you two going to be okay tonight?" In silence, we both turned around at the same time and waved our hands, bye-bye.

NINE

Momma

and Me

I was so tired when we got home that night, I didn't even remember falling asleep. I must have been asleep, though, because I woke up the next morning.

Yawning, I slowly cracked open one eye at a time. To my surprise, I wasn't in my own bed. Lying on my back, looking straight up at the ceiling, I could tell I was in my momma's bedroom.

How did I end up in Momma's bed? I wondered. I never sleep with Momma. Well, unless there's a really bad thunderstorm. Since we moved to Wakeview, I hadn't slept in Momma's bed not once.

I could hear Momma breathing peacefully beside me. "It must be raining hard this morning," I said to myself. That's the only reason I could come up with as to why Momma hadn't gone to work yet. So I lay still as a sleeping cat, listening for raindrops tapping against the windowpane.

That time in the early morning, there's no cars passing by on the highway out in front of my house. Everything is so still and peaceful, you can decide what you want your ears to hear. I could hear the motor of the icebox in the kitchen running. It was a steady hum. When the motor shut off, it was even totally more quiet.

The birds singing in nearby trees took turns singing. It was so quiet, I could almost tell which trees were occupied with that morning's singers. I could even tell the difference in the types of birds. Didn't know their names. Just knew how they looked and sounded.

It's wild being awake that time in the morning. One second, your eyes are open and it's still dark. Then it's like you're awake, right? Then, okay, you blink your eyes again and it's not dark anymore. You say to yourself, "Wow! The sun is up." It happens just that quick.

Momma rolled over on her side, facing me with her eyes wide open. I felt like I was on one of those slides you look at under a microscope. In science class last year, I remember we looked at a sample of pond water under a microscope. Lawrence Fisher, this tall, ugly guy in my class, found an amoeba on his slide. I was the only girl he let take a look. I kinda felt like that amoeba probably felt. Folks eyeballing and staring at it.

We both just lay there in bed facing each other. I reckon so much was said the night before, neither of us knew what to say. The telephone rang, startling us both. Momma quickly got up and ran to the kitchen to answer it. I went outside and discovered that the sun was shining. It wasn't raining and hadn't been, either. Why didn't Momma go to work? I wondered. I'd never known Momma to skip work.

Momma came out on the front porch. "That was Jonathan. He wants to know if we want to go fishing today," she said. She sat down beside me on the top step.

"Momma, ain't you going to work?" I mumbled. "I mean, I don't want you to go or anything. It's just you ain't never stayed home from work unless it was raining or I was really, really sick."

Momma twirled her finger around one of my pigtails. "I figured I should spend a little time with you today, considering what happened last night 'n all." She looked sad.

"What's the matter, Momma?" I asked. And Momma actually answered me.

"Oh, Sylvia. Lord knows everything is wrong. Me and sis, I mean, your real mother, we should have known that our secrets would eventually come out in the open."

Somehow, I felt closer to Momma than I'd ever felt before. I shifted my hips towards her. "What was she like?" I asked.

Momma looked down at her bare feet on the dusty porch steps. "Me and Sherry was identical twins. We looked almost exactly the same. The only real difference in us was the way we smiled or held our mouth. Folks really couldn't tell us

apart." Momma nodded her head with a little chuckle.

"Sherry loved singing and talking more than anything. In school, she used to get in the most trouble for running her mouth. I always dreamed of Sherry singing some place high and mighty, like on Broadway or Hollywood. She sho' could carry a tune, even without music. You ever heard of *a capella*? It means singing without music in the background. Sherry's group sang a capella because free musicians was hard to come by."

I didn't want to upset Momma, but I had to know. "Did she have a funeral? And did she have a funeral bulletin? Miz Lula Maye has boxes full of bulletins. Is her picture on the front?"

"Well, Sylvia," Momma said, "there was a funeral, but you were too young to remember. I couldn't afford to pay extra for bulletins. Besides, I wanted to remember her the way she was before she got sick." That sounded exactly like what Miz Lula Maye had said the other day when I was looking in her boxes.

Momma and me, we stayed locked up together on the front porch step for quite a while.

Somehow, I felt older. I mean, I'll be eleven in September. Just at that moment, though, I felt like I'd aged.

Later, Momma and me decided to take Mr. Jonathan up on his offer to go fishing. When we arrived to Miz Lula Maye's, Mr. Jonathan was standing at the screen door.

"Well, good morning again, ladies," said Mr. Jonathan in his proper-sounding voice. He opened the door and let us in.

Miz Lula Maye wasn't in the kitchen or the living room. I peeped in her bedroom and said, "Well, where is she?" Mr. Jonathan shook his head and laughed. "What?" I asked. "What's so funny?"

He quit laughing and explained, "Sylvia, you've got it, honest. You are just like your great-grandmother—inquisitive, full of questions, got to know stuff, got to know what's going on. I'm not laughing at you. It's just tickling me to see my grandmother coming out in you."

Mr. Jonathan grabbed an old ugly straw hat from Miz Lula Maye's front room closet. "Jack Jr.

and grandmother went to town. I'm guessing that they won't be back for a while. So, ladies, do I have a date?"

Oh my Lord, I thought, did he say *date*? I ain't never been on a date. I never dreamed of my first date being with my own daddy. Momma and me looked at each other. I think she thought his proper talk was as strange as I did. Two fishing rods leaned up against the wall beside the front door. I grabbed the shortest rod and opened the door.

"Well, come on you two," I said standing in the doorway with the screen door wide open. "We goin' fishin', but it's definitely not a date."

We walked through the fields and the forest in back of Miz Lula Maye's house. I discovered mosquito heaven on the way. The closer we got to Catfish Creek, the more mosquitoes attacked my bare legs. Despite the mosquitoes, the area around the creek was beautiful. We, well, Mr. Jonathan, did more talking than fishing. He sure does like to talk. I was kinda getting used to it.

I listened to Momma and Mr. Jonathan talk about Momma Sherry. It sounded to me like Mr. Jonathan had really loved her. For the first time,

I thought about how sad he must be that she died. Then I realized I never got around to asking Mr. Jonathan what he wanted me to call him. Well, now was as good a time as any, I decided. I was nervous, but I could also tell that the mood was a happy-peaceful kinda moment.

"Um, I have a question," I said looking at Mr. Jonathan. "I mean, can I ask you something?"

"Why sure, Sylvia, you may ask me anything in the world your pretty little heart desires," exclaimed Mr. Jonathan with a goofy-looking smile. I tried not to laugh, because for me, this was a very serious and important question. But he was some kinda funny.

"Okay, here goes," I whispered to myself. "What do you want me to call you?" I asked.

Mr. Jonathan smiled and motioned for me to sit down beside him on the ground. "This is some unfinished business. Well, to be honest, I had not thought about it. What name did you have in mind?"

I didn't want to decide. I wanted him to decide.

Momma said, "What about Dr. J, like the

greatest pro basketball star of all time?" We all laughed.

"What about Daddy J?" joked Mr. Jonathan.

Then I said in a serious voice, "What about Daddy?"

If I didn't know better, I'd have thought I saw tears growing in Mr. Jonathan's—oops! my daddy's eyes. And for once, my daddy had nothing to say.

Chapter **TEN**

Lemonade

We left the creek empty-handed, meaning no fish. But I didn't mind. Everything seemed to float. I don't think I've ever felt so good before. I kept floating until we got back to Miz Lula Maye's house.

"Have they gotten back yet?" I asked.

"Here they come now," said Mr. Jonathan. (This daddy thing will take some getting used to.)

I ran up on the porch with the cats and watched Jack Jr. drive up Pearle Road. A huge cloud of dust hung behind his car as if it was blowin' out smoke like a dragon. Jack Jr. was leanin' back in his raggedy old car like he was some cool dude. In his dreams, I thought. Jack Jr. was way too much of a nut to be a cool dude.

I questioned Jack Jr. about his whereabouts with Miz Lula Maye. Jack Jr. smiled with his stupid-looking self and said, "I'll let Auntie Maye do the honors." What was he up to now? I wondered. Jack Jr.'s always got somethin' going on.

"I'm not doin' any honors until I get something to drink. I'm parched," said Miz Lula Maye. "How 'bouts we make a pitcher of fresh lemonade?"

She asked my daddy to come and squeeze the lemons. Of course, she asked me to do the stirrin'. Miz Lula Maye says since I'm a beginner learning my way around the kitchen, that stirring and mixing are the best jobs for me. While you stirring and mixing up stuff, you can also watch and listen to her. Watching and listening is the way she learned how to cook. So that's the way she taught her daughters, and that's the way she's teaching me.

Miz Lula Maye was in charge of adding all the ingredients. First she poured some lukewarm water into a big glass jar called a pickle jar. It's

called a pickle jar 'cause that's what was originally in the jar when she bought it from the supermarket. She filled the pickle jar up about halfways. Then she added about a cup of sugar and said, "Stir it up, child."

To get the lemons soft enough to squeeze out the juice, Mr. Jonathan rolled each lemon back and forth, back and forth on the counter with the palm of his hand. Next he cut the tops off all the lemons and squeezed 'em as hard as he could over a bowl. Lemon juice came pouring out of the lemons like water from a water fountain.

I didn't hear Miz Lula Maye tellin' him to do anything. He automatically knew what to do. I guess Miz Lula Maye musta taught my daddy how to cook, too.

While Mr. Jonathan was squeezing the lemons, I whispered to Miz Lula Maye, "So you know about my real momma?"

Miz Lula Maye stopped wiping up the lemon juice mess Mr. Jonathan left on the counter. "I reckons I do, baby. Your daddy and I learned about everything during yesterday's storm. You alright, ain't ya?"

I nodded my head yes. So that's why Momma stopped by Miz Lula Maye's yesterday instead of coming straight home, I realized. She let the biggest secret of the summer out of its hole.

Mr. Jonathan carefully removed all of the seeds from the juice in the bowl. He cut up a few of the lemons and dropped 'em (peel and all) into the pickle jar with the sugar water. Miz Lula Maye said it again, "Stir it up, child. Stir it up good."

Mr. Jonathan poured the bowl of lemon juice into the pickle jar. Then Miz Lula Maye added a little more sugar after doing a taste test. She added cold water from the icebox along with a couple of ice cubes, filling the pickle jar up to the rim. It was ready.

Mr. Jonathan pulled some glasses down from the cabinet and filled 'em with ice. "Oops!" he said. "We almost forgot the best part. You remember what I like in my fresh lemonade?"

Miz Lula Maye smiled saying, "Uh-huh, sure do!"

I had no idea what they were talking about. Miz Lula Maye walked over to the cabinet where she keeps her spices and pulled out a jar of honey.

It was some dirty lookin' honey. Had stuff floatin' around in it. Honeycombs, I reckons.

Now, here they go, I thought to myself. They gettin' ready to mess up some perfectly good tastin' fresh lemonade.

Miz Lula Maye spooned up some honey and drizzled it over the ice in all of the glasses. Then she sprinkled a little brown sugar on top. "Don't do mine!" I said in a panic.

"It's good! Trust me. You'll like it," said Mr. Jonathan.

Miz Lula Maye motioned for Jack Jr. and Momma to have some lemonade. Jack Jr. popped up into the kitchen sayin', "Auntie Maye, you knows you ain't gotta ask me twice when it comes to your lemonade."

"Marie, come on in here and get you a glass," requested Miz Lula Maye.

We all went out front and sat on the porch. Of course, Jack Jr. had to aggravate Miz Lula Maye by teasing her cats. It was somethin' funny being amongst Jack Jr. and his foolishness.

Mr. Jonathan . . . I mean my daddy, was right. A little honey and brown sugar in fresh lemonade does taste good. It gets rid of the tartness. The honey makes the lemonade taste sweeter and smoother. I was so thirsty, I drank three glasses down straight.

In the middle of slurping on a piece of ice, Miz Lula Maye asked, "Marie, ain't it a blessing how the two of you ended up in Wakeview? Of all the places, you came right here to Pearle Road."

After Miz Lula Maye said that, a gust of wind seemed to blow in an unusual moment of silence. Momma had a weird look on her face, like something was biting at her nerves. She'd drank all of her lemonade, but the glass was still full of ice. Momma rubbed her forehead with the side of her cold glass. Then she began talking.

"I sho' hope ya'll will come to forgive me one day. It's hard to explain. I really thought I could manage things on my own. I'd kept the secret for so long, traveling around Florida getting whatever work I could get. After my last job pickin' oranges, I was fed up and used up. I remembered Sherry mentioning a place in South Carolina called Wakeview as being the place Jonathan was from. I figured Sylvia deserved better. So when school let out for the summer, we got on a bus and came." Momma paused and shook her head.

"Shucks, I thought I'd trust my luck. I didn't really know if anybody still lived here. Didn't know what to expect. I just stepped out on faith. I needed help that only family could provide.

"When we got here, everything seemed to fall right into place. I thought, Whew! Thank you Jesus! Maybe this was the right move. But when Jonathan showed up, I knew things were gonna change. I knew it wouldn't be long, I knew I couldn't keep the secrets much longer."

Momma hung her head real low. I could see she felt ashamed of herself. She knew exactly what she was doing when we moved to Wakeview. Momma took a chance for me, not knowing how things would turn out.

"You done right, Marie. You did the right thing by bringing Sylvia into our lives," Miz Lula Maye said. "Sylvia, you remember the map we found in one of my secret holes the other day? Well, it's sittin' on my dresser. Will you go and fetch it for me?"

I hopped right up and went inside. When I came back, I heard Miz Lula Maye tellin' Momma why she and Jack Jr. went into town.

Miz Lula Maye had gone to the courthouse to see about deeding the house and some land to me and Momma. Miz Lula Maye unfolded the map and stretched it out across her lap.

"Marie and Sylvia, all this here is yours," Miz Lula Maye said, pointing to a place on the map. "All of my children owns a piece of land. You've had a hard life. And I believes trouble shouldn't last always. Let's say the storm is over. And since you want to live here, you might as well own your own place."

Wow! I was speechless, in shock, and couldn't believe that somebody could ever be so giving. I was so happy, folks in North Carolina could see me grinning from ear to ear.

Momma started to say that she couldn't take Miz Lula Maye's offer, but Miz Lula Maye told her to "Hush up and stop talking nonsense." We all laughed at Miz Lula Maye settin' Momma straight. Like I've said a million times before, Miz Lula Maye doesn't mind setting ya straight.

Still Momma insisted, "This is too much. Maybe you should just put the house in Sylvia's name. Besides, she's your kin."

Miz Lula Maye had to set Momma straight again. "Now, you listen here, Marie. You's my kin, too! You been a momma to my great-grand-daughter all these years. The way I see it, that makes you my granddaughter. Now, I won't hear another word."

I ain't never seen Momma so happy in all of my life. She was a little bashful, but she went over to Miz Lula Maye and gave her a kiss on the cheek. "I don't know how to thank you," Momma said.

"You already have," Miz Lula Maye said with her cackling laugh. Then Miz Lula Maye stood up and hugged Momma like family.

I had an idea. "Hey, Jack Jr., will you do me a favor? Will you drive me home? I've got some-thing I want to show everybody." I couldn't believe it, but with no questions or wise com-ments, Jack Jr. did exactly what I asked.

For the rest of that afternoon, we sat on Miz Lula Maye's front porch working on my family tree. Miz Lula Maye helped the most. Even though Miz Lula Maye is one hundred years old, her memory is great.

We made a mess of my family tree, so Momma helped me make a new copy to hang on the wall in my room. She didn't have much family to add. For a second, that made me feel sad. But then I remembered that now Momma belongs to Miz Lula Maye (my great-grandma and bestest friend) just like I do. And then I didn't feel sad anymore.

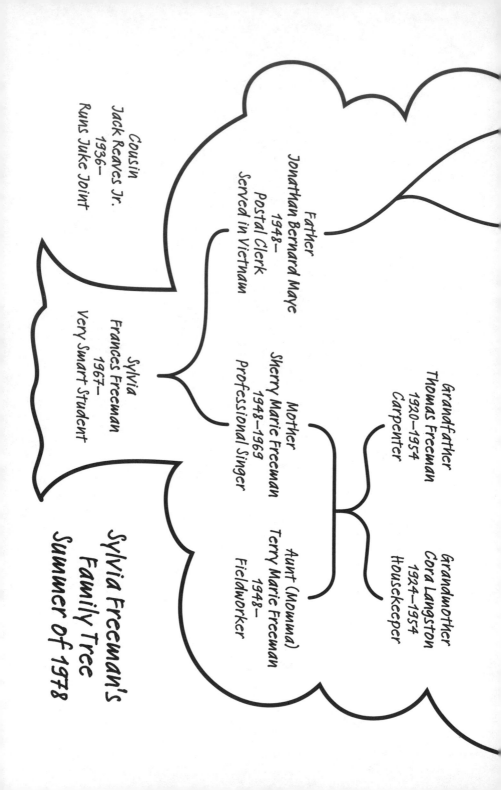

Cousin
Jack Reaves Jr.
1936–
Runs Juke Joint

Father
Jonathan Bernard Maye
1948–
Postal Clerk
Served in Vietnam

Sylvia
Frances Freeman
1967–
Very Smart Student

Grandfather
Thomas Freeman
1920–1954
Carpenter

Grandmother
Cora Langston
1924–1954
Housekeeper

Mother
Sherry Marie Freeman
1948–1969
Professional Singer

Aunt (Momma)
Terry Marie Freeman
1948–
Fieldworker

Sylvia Freeman's
Family Tree
Summer of 1978

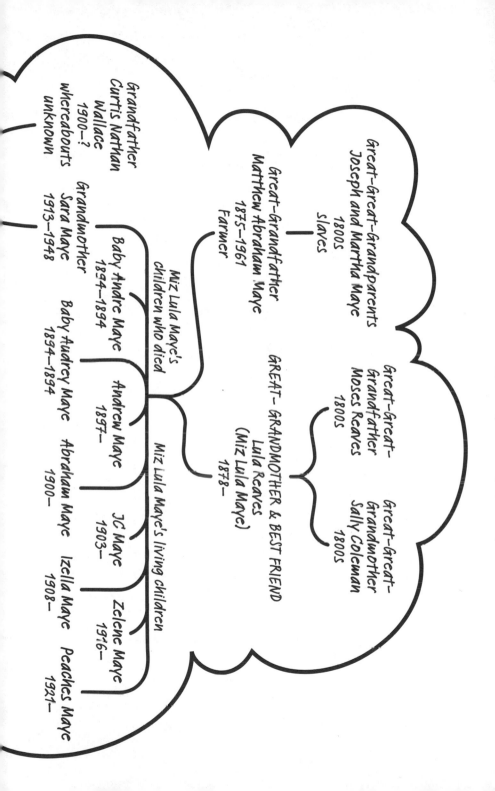

Grandfather
Curtis Nathan
Wallace
1900–?
whereabouts
unknown

Grandmother
Sara Maye
1913–1948

Great-Great-Grandparents
Joseph and Martha Maye
1800s
slaves

Great-Grandfather
Matthew Abraham Maye
1875–1961
Farmer

Miz Lula Maye's
children who died

Baby Andre Maye
1894–1894

Baby Audrey Maye
1894–1894

Great-Great-Grandfather
Moses Reaves
1800s

Great-Great-Grandmother
Sally Coleman
1800s

GREAT-GRANDMOTHER & BEST FRIEND
Lula Reaves
(Miz Lula Maye)
1878–

Andrew Maye
1897–

JC Maye
1903–

Zelene Maye
1916–

Abraham Maye
1900–

Izella Maye
1908–

Peaches Maye
1921–

Miz Lula Maye's living children

ACKNOWLEDGMENTS

First and foremost, I'd like to thank my immediate family for their love, support, and patience. I love you, Merrill, Jasmine, and Joey. Thank you, Momma, for teaching and showing me how to be strong and brave. Thanks to my sisters (Ernestine, Gwen, and Patricia) and brothers (George, Glenn, and Tony) for your love and support. Also, thanks to my other families and friends for spreading the word about my book from coast to coast. All of you know who you are. Thanks also to the people at Cornerstone and Central.

Thanks to the folks at East Carolina University's School of Health and Human Performance for supporting an alumna. Also, a special thank you to the librarians, teachers, and students of the many schools I've visited for choosing me and my work. Thanks, Nikki Giovanni, for your kind words and offerings of wisdom.

I'd also like to express many thanks to the people I work with every day at E.B. Aycock Middle School. Thanks to all the people affiliated with Carolrhoda Books. My editor, Vicki Liestman, deserves special thanks for all she has done and still does for me. "Kudos" once again are in order for my illustrator Felicia Marshall. Last, but certainly not least, thanks to my readers for reading my work and showing interest in a newcomer.

Pansie Hart Flood was born in Wilmington, North Carolina. After graduating from East Carolina University, she became a teacher. She lives in Greenville, North Carolina, with her husband and two children. She is also the author of *Sylvia & Miz Lula Maye*, which *School Library Journal* called a "satisfying and humorous" first novel.

Felicia Marshall has illustrated several books for children, including *Sylvia & Miz Lula Maye* and *Moaning Bones: African-American Ghost Stories*. She teaches art in Houston, Texas, where she lives with her husband and son.